Worthy and Worth It

Samantha Gail B. Lucas

Ukiyoto Publishing

All global publishing rights are held by

Ukiyoto Publishing

Published in 2024

Content Copyright © Samantha Gail B. Lucas

ISBN 9789361725562

*All rights reserved.
No part of this publication may be reproduced,
transmitted, or stored in a retrieval system, in any form
by any means, electronic, mechanical, photocopying,
recording or otherwise, without the prior permission of
the publisher.*

The moral rights of the authors have been asserted.

*This book is sold subject to the condition that it shall not by
way of trade or otherwise, be lent, resold, hired out or
otherwise circulated, without the publisher's prior
consent, in any form of binding or cover other than that in
which it is published.*

www.ukiyoto.com

Acknowledgments

I would like to thank my mother, Cheryl, and my late father, Mario, for investing in my education and encouraging me to follow my dreams.

I would also like to thank my partner Miguel Lopez for always rooting for me.

I would also like to thank everyone who supported me and my books. Thank you for also buying a copy of this book! I hope your kindness will be returned to you tenfold.

Introduction

The idea to write this book occurred to me during a challenging time in my life. A few of my plans were cancelled due to circumstances beyond my control. I was able to get over these changes in my schedule, but I felt sad because of some plans which were no longer happening. To cheer myself up, I went out, ate a good meal, and watched a movie. I went home happy and full. And it was during this moment that I realized that I was able to make myself happy, because I knew that I was worth it.

No matter what factors in my life will change, I am still able to find my footing and go with the flow. I believe that this is possible because I know that I am worthy of happiness. I know that I am worth fighting for, even if I am facing challenges and uncertainties.

As long as I am sure of myself, I can solve my own problems and make life worth living.

I hope that this book of essays can help you navigate through life with your head held high. Life is never easy. We all have our own problems to overcome. There are bad days which will remind us of the good days that will come afterwards. And there are days when we simply feel off. But it is possible to find joy amidst all of life's uncertainties. As long as you believe in yourself, you will realize that you are worthy of joy and inner peace.

Maybe you are feeling lost and insecure. I have been there a lot in the past. In fact, I still feel lost and insecure sometimes. But I do not let these feelings stop me from fulfilling my goals and writing my books. I use my insecurities to challenge myself. I try my best to improve myself. I do what I can to make my life better. I do this every single day. And to my delight, I am able to accept myself for who I am, even during bad days.

There is always a reason why you should feel proud of yourself. And I am not talking about your physical appearance alone. In fact, what matters most is who you are on the inside. In this book, I will share how I gained confidence and realized that I am worthy of being the best that I can be. It started by acknowledging my strengths and weaknesses. I became self-aware, and this led me to work on myself. This is an everyday process, and I am happy to share that it can be done by everyone. You just have to trust in yourself.

You can have everything that your heart desires, but if you do not feel worthy of them, then everything will be meaningless. You have to believe that you are worthy. You have to know that you are worth it. And if you are happy with yourself, you can enjoy the fruits of your labor and the company of your loved ones.

So join me as I help you feel *Worthy and Worth It!*

Contents

I Stopped Hating Myself	1
I Acknowledged My Flaws	4
I Acknowledged My Own Strengths	7
I Forgave Myself	10
I Focused on Myself	13
I Invested in My Health	16
I Happily Dined Alone	19
I Worked for Myself	22
I Became Thankful	25
I Said Goodbye to Toxic People	28
I Wrote My Own Story	32
I Learned to Let Go	35
I Gave Myself the Chance to Be Happy	38
I Became My Own Partner	41
I Shared My Blessings	44
About the Author	*47*

I Stopped Hating Myself

The first step to believing in yourself is to stop hating yourself. When I stopped hating myself, I felt that the world was instantly a better place for me. I also realized that I was capable of being kind to myself. Self-love is the key to being worth it.

I used to hate myself for not meeting some of the beauty standards of my society. I tried very hard to fit in, but it was frustrating. It left me feeling empty inside. Everything changed when I opted to appreciate my own unique looks and to stop conforming to society's unrealistic standards. Instead of being too hard on myself, I embraced my face and body. There is only one me, and I chose to work with what I had. Now, I express myself through fashion and self-confidence. Loving myself was the first step to being able to carry myself well.

Once I felt good about myself, I started to embrace myself for who I really am. I used to berate myself for not being good with numbers, for not being the most outgoing person, and for choosing to live a quiet life instead of an immensely successful yet public one. But then, I realized that there is power in my words, so I became a published author. There is freedom in being an observer, so I chose to watch the people around me. This has become my inspiration for my books. I also appreciated my quiet life, which lets me enjoy the things that I love, such as reading and writing. Once I loved myself, I knew that I was unstoppable. I was worthy of happiness. And when I am facing my own challenges, I know that my experiences have prepared me to handle them with wisdom and action.

I know that hating myself was harmful, because I became negative towards myself and those around me. But when I learned to love myself, I became kinder and more patient with myself. I became friendlier and more approachable. I appreciated my skills, and I was able to work more efficiently and effectively. I learned to be happy with my successes and failures. And I became excited for the future, because I know that I am worthy of a bright one ahead.

If you still find it difficult to love yourself, I suggest that you stop. Stop with all the noise in your head. Stop and simply pause. Take a deep breath. Listen to what your body is saying. Chances are, you are simply tired. You need to take a breather and reflect on why you are worthy of love. There is always something that will make you feel better about yourself. For instance, you know that you have a lovely smile. You know that you can communicate with ease and confidence. Now, start with those traits and work on them. Operate from a place of self-love, and you will eventually build your confidence and trust in yourself.

Stop hating yourself, and instead, start winning in life because you are definitely worth it!

I Acknowledged My Flaws

Once I was able to love myself, I used journaling to help me acknowledge my flaws. The first step was to believe in myself, and in my ability to make it in this world. Next, I reassured myself that I am not required to be perfect. It is important for me to know that it is impossible to be perfect, because society can have unrealistic expectations. Once I was aware that it was alright for me to thrive while being an imperfect human being, I was able to acknowledge my flaws and limitations.

I started with the obvious ones, which were the traits that I have struggled with since I was young. Most of them were on the inside, and I had limiting beliefs which prevented me from starting my journey as a published author earlier in my life. While I have no regrets in starting my writing career in my 30s, I know that by acknowledging my flaws, I am giving myself the opportunity to succeed in other areas of my life at the right time. I wrote this process down in my journal. I reflected on the necessary actions to take in order to work with my flaws. I realized that now that I am in my 30s, it is easier to work with my flaws. I no longer have to succumb to my insecurities because I am aware that I can figure out my way through life. And with my own experiences, I am able to know that my flaws can help me keep myself in check in a fast-paced world.

I hope that journaling about your flaws can help you acknowledge them. Start with the ones that have been seemingly weighing you down for years, and make peace with them. Next, use the lessons from your own experiences to create means and solutions for living with these flaws. The simplest solutions such as daily journaling and working out can help you live with your insecurities and limitations. While your insecurities will not disappear overnight, it is important that you eventually learn how to live with them. The time will come when you will realize that you are worthy of self-love, and that will come when you are able to acknowledge the limitations that make you human.

Your journey to being worthy of happiness starts when your flaws no longer feel like shackles and when your insecurities no longer cripple you. You can walk with your head held high because you respect yourself and you acknowledge that you do not need to be perfect. You can get through everything through your skills and abilities. Your flaws do not need to stop you from moving forward.

You are worthy of having a good life because you do not need to be perfect. Everyone has flaws and insecurities, and everyone has the opportunity to overcome them. Start by journaling and writing down ways on how you can live with them.

Yes, you can empower yourself because you are worth it. Live your best life today!

I Acknowledged My Own Strengths

Once I was able to acknowledge my weaknesses, I moved on to my strengths. Growing up, I was trained in school to be modest when it came to my strengths. But as I became an adult, I learned that celebrating the strengths that make me shine is empowering. There is a way to acknowledge my strengths without being boastful. In fact, I believe that by celebrating the traits that make me shine, I am inspiring myself and others to do well in life. So, I decided to make this a priority, and I started with journaling.

I used my journal to list down my strengths. One of them is writing. I am passionate about writing, and this book is proof of that. I am able to inspire others through my written essays, books, and blog entries. I am also able to share my experiences through the written word. What began as a hobby eventually became my career. So, I owe my life to writing, and I hope that more people will use their greatest strength to propel themselves forward.

Another strength of mine that I chose to celebrate was my determination to succeed. I always drove myself to excel in my work and in my personal life. I chose to work hard, and I applied my skills in the process. I also asked for help in order to learn and improve myself. I never stopped learning, and I knew that success is not something that I can achieve by myself. Even writing this book is a team effort between me and my publisher. Now that you are able to read this book, you are also a part of my success, and I thank you for choosing this book to help you grow.

The third strength that I celebrated was my ability to choose happiness each day. Even when times were hard, I still focused on the simple joys that made me smile. I knew that while life is challenging, there will always be a reason to be happy everyday. I appreciated my simple joys more when everything seemed to be falling apart, and I also became grateful for them when everything was falling into place. I am glad that my ability to be happy has inspired me to have an abundance mindset.

I still have more strengths to celebrate, but I chose to focus on these three to keep myself going. I chose to inspire myself by remembering that my strengths have allowed me to have a good life, and they will continue to let me achieve more things in the future. I hope that as you remember your top three strengths and list them down in your journal, you will also realize how far you have come, and how much you can still achieve. You also have what it takes to have a wonderful life, because you are worthy of abundance and success.

Use your strengths to inspire yourself, especially during difficult times. You can be your own inspiration, and you are worthy of inspiring not just yourself, but others around you as well.

I Forgave Myself

It was easy for me to acknowledge my flaws and strengths. I got to know myself very well through journaling, and I wanted to take a step further in improving myself. So, I made time to assess my own faults and worked towards forgiving myself.

The first step to doing so was to be aware of my own mistakes. I have discussed this already in my previous books, but it still feels challenging to write about forgiving myself. Still, there were some practices which made the process possible. Allow me to share them with you.

Self-awareness goes a long way in forgiving myself. I knew that there were actions in the past which I particularly regret because I did not give them much thought. Looking back, I know that I could have done better in order to avoid hurting myself. I may have offended some people, and I am sorry for that. I have already asked forgiveness from those I have hurt, and they did say that they had their own faults too. It was easy for me to forgive them for their own wrongdoings because I have already forgiven myself. I am also forgiving myself for the mistakes which were unintentional and for those which have affected other people. I know that all of my mistakes have affected me the most, especially since I am now aware that I could have done better. I continue to journal about my past mistakes and I am also applying what I have learned as I write my books. Indeed, there is a lot that I can do out of the lessons I have learned, and I am proud to share them with my readers and friends.

Once I was able to forgive myself, I felt lighter on the inside. I felt free. I felt worthy of pursuing my passions and chasing my dreams. I felt capable of working towards my goals and helping others in the process. I realized that I was capable of making things possible. Forgiving myself has helped me forgive others too, and it has allowed me to collaborate with others with a more open mind and a wider understanding of the world. Since I know that there is no need for me to be perfect, I can acknowledge that my mistakes and the wrongdoings of others are simply part of life. We all need to experience mistakes in order to learn, grow up, and improve ourselves. So, forgiveness is an essential part of being the best version of yourself.

- It is important to reward yourself after genuinely forgiving yourself. Of course, the best reward is the lightness and freedom that you feel in your heart. But it will also be helpful if you can treat yourself to a nice meal, or if you can buy yourself a treat for getting over a major milestone such as self-forgiveness. Know that this is simply one of the important steps that you need to take as you live your life, and there will be more instances like this in the future. You are simply learning how to live life better, and rewarding yourself means that you understand the lessons that life throws at you.

Keep on forgiving yourself, and experience the joy of being worthy of the best life that you can give to yourself.

I Focused on Myself

I was determined to focus on myself and my own well-being once I realized that I owed it to myself to be the best that I can be. In order to become the best version of myself, I continued to journal about my aspirations and plans for the future. I realized that I could make my dreams come true with hard work and determination. So, I stopped comparing myself to others and listened to my heart. I pursued my passions as I focused on myself.

Comparing myself to others did more harm than good in the past. I only went down a self-destructive path which not only derailed my plans, but also made me believe that I was not worthy of success and happiness. I overcame my tendency to compare myself to others by writing down ten things that I was grateful for each day. It may sound simple, but it actually worked for me! By highlighting the blessings that I was receiving everyday, I realized that I was capable of making good things happen in my life. I also prayed for more blessings, and I worked hard to fulfill my goals. I started to believe in myself, and it became clear to me that I had everything I needed to live the life that I have always wanted.

Focusing on myself has also helped me become happier for other people's success. I knew how hard it was to reach significant milestones, and watching the people around me succeed inspires me to also be successful. This does not mean that I am comparing myself to them. I am simply happy for the people who have made their own dreams come true.

I used the inspiration that I got from watching people succeed and from being grateful for my own blessings to work hard. I focused on my priorities and showed up to my plans. I stopped feeling resentful for missed opportunities because I chose to be where I am today. These opportunities were simply not for me, and I made the right choice to stick to the ones which were definitely for me. If you are experiencing some rejections, know that everyone goes through them. These rejections will not only teach you valuable lessons, but they will also show you how to improve yourself. Learn to let go and move forward so that you can focus on the other opportunities that life has in store for you.

Focusing on yourself is not selfish. You can help others better if you are able to meet your own needs and achieve your goals. You will only feel worth it if you make yourself your number one priority. You can make your own dreams come true if you work hard and reward yourself. Never forget that self-worth is built on acknowledging your strengths as you work on your areas of weakness.

Focus on yourself by competing with yourself and being grateful for what you have. The rest will follow, and you will have everything that you have always wanted.

I Invested in My Health

Taking care of my health has taken center stage during the pandemic. I took extra precautions to fortify my immunity. I worked out during the lockdown, which has already been my everyday routine even before the pandemic. I lived a more balanced life. Once I made my own health a priority, I became more at peace with myself, and yes, I felt worth it of being in the best state of health.

Being healthy also means having being mentally balanced. I make sure that I know myself well, and I am able to help myself during difficult times. Once I became confident in myself, I wrote self-help books to help others who are going through the common issues that everyone faces in life. I became a voice for the countless people who are improving themselves while working and thriving during uncertain times. Writing has improved my outlook in life, as well as my work ethic. I know that my books can encourage others to take better care of themselves, and I use my own knowledge to help myself as well.

Being in shape allows me to think things through in a more balanced way. I truly believe that my workouts have helped me cope physically and mentally with the challenges that I have faced in the past. Since I know how effective my daily workouts are, I will continue to do them so that I can be strong not just for myself, but for my future family as well. I want to continue being fit and in great shape so that I can live longer for the ones I love.

I believe that I am worthy of being healthy. The only way for me to honor my mind and body is to take care of myself. I have been through tough times which made me cope in negative ways, and I know that many people go through rough patches as well. But I know now that the best way to cope with life's challenges is through self-care and a healthy lifestyle. I may not have done anything illegal in the past, but I failed to honor my mind and body by living an unhealthy lifestyle before. It took a global pandemic for me to focus on my health and to take care of myself. I know by now that self-care is not just a fad. Rather, it is a lifestyle, and a healthier one at that. I will continue to take care of myself so that I can be the best version of myself for more years to come.

You can start taking care of yourself by working out for thirty minutes a day. Drink eight glasses of water. Get sufficient sleep. Read books that can feed your mind and educate yourself. Work on something that is bigger than yourself so that you can find meaning in life. Always be curious and mindful.

Health is so much more than your body. Try to live a balanced life so that you can have a healthy lifestyle.

I Happily Dined Alone

I enjoyed eating by myself so much that I wrote my book, *Happily Dining Alone*, about my own experiences. I wanted to share the joys of solo dining to the world, especially to my fellow Filipinos. You see, I live in the Philippines, and the society that I belong to can be critical of solo diners. This is especially true when it comes to women solo diners. I often get questioned where my partner is, or why I am dining alone. Well, I do enjoy eating by myself, and that does not necessarily mean that I dislike being with my partner. In fact, I feel recharged after my solo dining adventures, and this makes me a better partner. So, I hope that you will also give solo dining a try.

I get some of my best ideas for my books and for my projects while dining alone. There is something magical about spending time by myself just to eat a meal. I get to savor the food. I get to appreciate the ambience of the restaurant. I get to study the menu. I get to people-watch. I even read a book while enjoying my meal. It is quite a feast for the senses.

Another reason why I often eat by myself is because it is liberating. It is a refreshing take on life, especially since I live in a conservative society. I get to enjoy my meal without being distracted. I get to think of my priorities. I get to enjoy my own company. Appreciating my own company has reinforced my belief that I am worthy of happiness. I would not trade it for anything.

I suggest that you give solo dining a try. It is fun, and less intimidating than you think. Choose a restaurant that serves your comfort food. Bring a book, or listen to a podcast. The key is to make yourself feel comfortable. If you are not comfortable being alone, that is totally fine. You will get used to it. You can even write while waiting for your order. In fact, I wrote some chapters of my books while dining alone! Eating alone can get you in the zone, and I am sure you will enjoy it once you get used to it.

The best part about dining alone is that you will be able to discover new flavors by yourself. And I think that the best part of life is discovering what makes you happy. What can make you happy is totally up to you, and it is best to learn this alone. You can surely learn new things about yourself while savoring delicious meals when you eat out alone. It is also the perfect time and place to reflect on your journey through life, and what else you would like to pursue. Now, who says that eating out is a shallow endeavor? You can make it a time of reflection and self-discovery as you progress through life.

Give it a try, and you will not regret it!

I Worked for Myself

I have worked in the corporate world for many years before I gained the confidence to pursue writing full-time. I have always kept a roster of clients for freelance work, and I was fortunate to continue working for them once I left my former employer. It was challenging at the beginning because I was used to having a fixed schedule. Eventually, I learned to cope and enjoy having my own time to fulfill my tasks.

My freelance career has especially been helpful during the lockdown. The pandemic has forced everyone to stay at home 24/7, and writing has been one of the main reasons that I survived this period. I was able to write while volunteering as a crocheter of earsavers for frontline healthcare workers. It was also during this time that I launched my career as a published author. I learned how to master the art of writing for an audience, and I applied this to writing my self-help books. Now, my books are sold worldwide. I am grateful for my career as a published author.

Working for myself has given me the opportunity to assess my skills objectively. Since I work by myself, I need to ensure that I submit quality work all the time. To make sure that I am capable of being effective at my job, I continuously read and upskill through workshops, webinars, and books. I listen to feedback from my stakeholders and clients. When I transitioned to being a published author, I worked with editors, proofreaders, and my publishers to improve the quality of my work. All of these steps have helped me improve my writing. I became a professional writer, and not just someone who writes for fun. It was during this time that writing became not just my job, but also my passion and purpose in life.

I am happy to say that you do not need to work freelance in order to work for yourself. You can do this even if you are employed. Use your skills to create new opportunities for yourself in your job. Use your knowledge to improve, and constantly find new ways to become better everyday. Talk to your colleagues and learn from them. Make time for self-improvement, and use this time to grow holistically. You will experience changes in your career, but your skills and knowledge will stay with you forever. This is why you should always work for yourself, because you believe in yourself.

My books are just some of the reading materials that can help you become effective in your job. Self-help books will equip you with life lessons that will allow you to navigate through life with ease. Of course, these books will not work unless you do. Apply the lessons that you have learned to become effective in what you do. And maybe, you can also write your own book about your valuable experiences so that you can help others in the future.

You are worthy of being commended for your work, so make sure that you are delivering quality results all the time!

I Became Thankful

Another secret to feeling worthy of a good life is to be thankful for what you have. I used to live without gratitude, and I felt as if I was struggling all the time. Everything changed when I learned how to be grateful for what I have.

I started by keeping a gratitude journal, where I wrote ten things that I was grateful for each day. Eventually, I noticed the change in my mood and my overall happiness. I was still struggling in some aspects of my life, but I was no longer weighed down by my worries. I let my blessings uplift my spirit and improve my mindset.

Being thankful does not happen overnight. I understand that it may take some time to be grateful for what you have, especially if you are going through something overwhelming such as grief. You can talk to people whom you trust to help you with your gratitude journey. You do not need to do this alone.

Talk to them about the blessings which you might have overlooked, and ask for help in some areas of your life. Gratitude will eventually follow when you appreciate what you have as they happen to you.

Another way to feel grateful is to honor yourself during your important milestones. This is especially true if you do not have people to celebrate with you. Remember that you are not alone because you have yourself. Celebrate by eating alone at a restaurant, and buy something special for yourself. You deserve to treat yourself whenever you achieve great things, and use these experiences to inspire you to work hard and feel thankful for what you have.

Lastly, share what you have. Giving your time and treasure to others can be the most meaningful way to celebrate yourself and your resources. Give others the chance to have a delicious meal, the access to education, or resources which can improve their lives. You were able to make it this far because you persevered. Use your blessings to make a difference in the lives of others.

When life is too much for you to bear, remember that your blessings are still there in your life. The world does not owe you anything, but you are still blessed. Be thankful for the simple things that enable you to have a good life. Be grateful for what you have and what you can still share with others. Be grateful that you can read this book and you can tell others about what you have learned from it. Be thankful for the gift of life, and the work that you do.

Now, be the reason why others feel the same way. Be a blessing to others. Use your network to help others in their careers. Use your time to make others happy. Use your money to help others have a better life.

Be a blessing to yourself, and to others. Be grateful for what you have, and others around you will be thankful for what you have done in this world so far.

I Said Goodbye to Toxic People

Knowing my own self-worth has given me the courage to say goodbye to toxic people. This was not easy because most of them were people whom I have known all my life. But I had to do this for my own peace of mind. Now, I am happy that I let go of them because I was able to focus on my strengths and work on my weaknesses.

I started by journaling about the people who were not treating me well. They always said negative remarks to me, even when I was doing my best to reach my goals and fulfill my dreams. When I reached the milestones in my career, they still had negative comments which not only offended me but also confirmed my observation that they did not wish the best for me. They were intentionally mean and cruel, and I knew that I deserved better than that. So, I wrote down the ways that I could avoid them. I listed down the people whom to avoid for good, and I wrote down why I needed to do this. It was important for me to assess the situation with each toxic person. I needed to understand why letting them go would do me good, especially in the long run. I did not let them go simply because of one bad instance. Rather, it was a lifetime of negativity and hate that caused me to say goodbye to them.

I started by blocking them on social media. I am glad that there is the option to block those people who are no longer good for me. Next, I planned how my life would be without these people. I knew that it was easy to live life without them, but of course, there were occasions which they used to be a part of. So, I simply planned on going to places without them. I did not miss them on special occasions. In fact, it was refreshing to celebrate special events without people who were constantly mean to me. These people have no place in my life.

Letting toxic people go has given me the time and energy to focus on myself. I no longer devoted energy to processing my feelings towards them. I no longer had to be mindful of meeting their unrealistic expectations. Instead, I just focused on my life, career, and growth.

Since blocking these toxic people, I was able to believe in myself more. I was able to see the value of hard work, and I began appreciating myself more. Instead of feeling miserable whenever I was questioned for my hard work and being on the receiving end of their wrath and disappointment, I realized that it was better to live life being proud of myself and my own work. People who cannot be happy for me will never be happy for me. And most importantly, they can never be happy and content in their own lives.

I still get negative comments, but I no longer mind them because they do not come from people close to me. I only blocked those who used to be in my life, yet still chose to pull me down through their hurtful remarks. I only let go of toxic people, and I understand that the world is still a cruel place. It is up to me to choose my battles and to keep going on amidst the challenges that I face.

I know that I am worthy of a good life, and I strive to continue making each day count by myself, for myself.

I Wrote My Own Story

I began to write my own stories when I was still in high school. I was part of the school paper back then, and it was during this time that I received formal training in Creative Writing for the very first time. It was a magical experience because I felt as if I found the craft that I wanted to practice for the rest of my life. Now that I am in my 30s, I am a published author of multiple books. I was able to write my own story, and I made my high school writing dreams come true.

I wrote my own story because I learned during my training in high school that my forte was nonfiction writing. While I was also capable of writing fiction, I excelled more in writing about my own life experiences. This awareness was very important to me. It drove me to pursue further education in writing, as I pursued a Humanities degree in college. My rigorous training in the Liberal Arts has paved the way for more exposure to writing and various forms of literature. By the time I graduated from uni, I knew that writing was the career path for me.

However, life took over and I needed to find a more practical job. So, I devoted several years of my life to the financial sector. I was trained to follow a daily routine, and I was able to acquire the discipline of work. I value my years in the corporate world because I became adept at showing up for myself and working for something that was bigger than myself. I also learned how to observe different kinds of people. It was during my corporate career that I also knew that I would eventually end up being a writer. After working and moving up the corporate ladder, I became a full-time freelance writer. This career move became a source of inspiration and fulfillment for me. It has also sustained me during the pandemic, and it provided me with the opportunity to become a published writer during the lockdown.

Ideally, it would have been nice to pursue a career in Creative Writing upon graduation. But that did not happen to me, and I am grateful for the many detours in life which paved the way for me to write full-time. While I am not closing my doors to returning to the corporate world, I can say now that I am fortunate enough to know what I want to do for the rest of my life. Writing books is my passion, and creative nonfiction is my speciality. Someday, I will look back on those times when I decided to write full-time and eventually publish my books. I wrote my own story because I believed in myself and my own talents. I knew that I had what it takes to succeed, and I worked hard to make it all happen.

I hope that you can have the courage to pursue your dreams. Know that you are worthy of fulfilling your dreams and ambitions. Strive hard to make them come true, and live life to the fullest! Life is too short to live your life for others. This time, strive to make it for yourself.

I Learned to Let Go

I have always struggled with being accepted by other people. It has always been an uphill battle for me, especially when I was looking for validation from others. I was always too loud, too inquisitive, too productive, or too flashy. It seemed as if I could never fit in anywhere. This has caused me to feel unhappy for many years, until I resolved to simply let go. It was one of the best decisions I have ever made, and it has made me realize that it is easy to live my life on my own terms.

When I let go of people who never seemed to be happy for me, I had to make myself understand that I should learn to be happy on my own. I know that I never intended to offend or hurt anyone with my life. One example of this was my pixie cut, which was my hairstyle for many years. In the Philippines, having a pixie cut caused people to question my identity. In my conservative society, my pixie cut became problematic. However, I had this hairstyle because it was easy to maintain and it gave me an edgy look. I received negative comments about my hair almost everyday, and it affected me for years. One day, I just decided to stop caring about people's comments on my hair. Then, I decided to grow my hair again and I donated my hair to cancer patients once it reached the required length. One thing I learned from my hair journey is that this is just hair. It will grow back. It is simply a replaceable part of myself and it is no way tied to my identity. It is simply a style statement which helped me learn how to let go.

I also learned to let go by focusing on my books. Again, people had different opinions on my books. A lot of people I knew did not like my decision to release them internationally through Amazon and other retailers instead of selling them in local bookstores. Instead of feeling sad because of their opinions, I felt motivated to continue writing and promoting my books. People will always have different perspectives on my growth and career. They will never understand my struggles when I was starting out as a writer, and they will never appreciate my hard work because their idea of success is seeing a product on shelves near them. I will never be able to please them, so I just let go of them. I focused on my career, and I continued working hard. Now, I am happier and more fulfilled both personally and professionally.

Maybe you have several unresolved issues which are holding you back from letting go. I strongly recommend that you simply let go. This is the first step in order to resolve your issues and control your own life again. You should also work on your self-esteem and remind yourself that you are worthy of respect and love. You will never be happy unless you give yourself permission to thrive and excel.

Stop listening to others and focus on yourself. Focus on your work. Continue doing what you love, and just let go. You will be rewarded with genuine happiness and the courage to live the life you want.

I Gave Myself the Chance to Be Happy

It was during my darkest moments that I was able to find the solutions to my problems. I was grieving the death of my loved ones as I was balancing a writing career and volunteer work. One day, I just realized that focusing on my problems would not solve them. Instead, I realized that I should do things to improve myself.

There were many issues in my life which were beyond my control, such as the Covid-19 pandemic and grief. But I could control my attitude and approach to whatever life throws at me. So, I focused on self-improvement and resolved to give myself the chance to be happy.

My first priority in order to make happiness not just a possibility but a priority was to make my writing dreams come true. I already have experience as a freelance writer, but I also wanted to become a published author. So, I used my extra time at home during the pandemic to write my books. This is already my seventeenth book, and making my dream come true has made me very happy. I worked hard, but I also used my imagination and creativity to think of concepts for my books and to write them well. I am thankful for the opportunities that were given to me, and I continue to write books which would not only allow me to share my stories, but could also help others solve their problems.

My next solution was to give others the chance to help me. Help came in various forms. When I released my books, people who believed in me purchased them. When I had a book signing, those who were close to me showed up. When I needed a friend, I knew who to call. When I simply needed to take a break, I went out with my partner and my friends. It is important to know that while I am capable of helping myself, I am also letting others assist and support me. Giving people the chance to extend their kindness towards me has been a game changer for me. It made me realize that I am not alone in this world. And it is true that happiness is something that we should pass on to others.

The best solution to my problems was when I stopped caring about what other people thought about me. Their opinions do not matter to me anymore, because I know in my heart that I am doing my best and I am presenting the best version of myself. People who do not know what they are doing and saying can blurt out opinions which do not have any effect on me. I will only ask for the opinions of people who truly care about me. Those who have nothing nice to say can keep on saying hateful things, but they will never bring me down.

I hope that you can also give yourself the chance to be happy. Fulfill your own dreams, allow others to help you, and stop caring about what others think. You are your own person. It is time that your happiness should be on your terms, at your own pace, and at your own time.

I Became My Own Partner

I learned that the secret to happiness is to become my own partner. I have had many relationships in the past, and all of them failed because I did not know what I wanted for myself. So, when my last relationship failed, I worked on myself. I even wrote my book *Breaking Up Forward*, which was all about moving on after I left my former partner. It was during this time that I learned that in order to have a better relationship moving forward, I should learn how to become my own partner.

I read my previous journal entries, and I learned that the best way to keep myself grounded was to surround myself with books. I kept on reading, and this sustained me. Writing for a living meant that I needed to keep myself updated with the current trends in self-help and creative nonfiction, which were the two genres that I focused on.

Next, I dated myself. I regularly ate out a lot, and these lunches and dinners became opportunities for me to write a few chapters, listen to podcasts, and simply observe the people around me. I enjoyed eating out so much that I wrote my books *Happily Dining Alone* and *Date Yourself First* about my foodie adventures. Learning how to be comfortable as I ate and worked alone was important to me. I became more independent and self-assured. Most of all, I trusted my own judgement and I did not expect others to decide for me.

I simply relied on myself. This has helped me become my own person when I met my current partner. I no longer relied on him for major life decisions. I continued to write and work on my books. I carried on with my interests and I continued to read books that captured my imagination. I indulged in movies and watched concerts. I lived the life that I have always wanted for myself.

You just need to take a step back and observe what really matters to you. It is not difficult to become your own partner. You simply have to support yourself. You have to become capable of deciding for yourself, and you must have a voice in your community. Find your tribe, but learn to speak for yourself. When you are alone, you have to learn to enjoy your own company. You need to stop feeling incomplete when you are alone. You must learn how to be fulfilled by yourself.

I wish that I learned how to become my own partner earlier in life. I could have been spared from the emptiness that I felt when I had no idea where to go as far as my own journey was concerned. When I made myself my number one priority, I found a partner who respected me and my boundaries. Having my own thing is crucial in growing as a person and with my partner.

I am worthy of being the best partner for myself, as well as the best partner that I can be for the one who chose to be with me.

I Shared My Blessings

I remember being broke and sad in college after breaking up with my former partner. Our relationship was not working out, and I needed a reset. After laying low for a few months, I decided to sponsor a child's education through an organization for a year. It was a monthly commitment that I was drawn to because the fees made me responsible for a child's education and welfare for an affordable rate. After a few months, I became involved with my sponsored child's life through regular correspondence and updates. I also saw my resources as a way to share my blessings. Sure, I still had limited resources, but knowing that I was capable of improving someone else's life in my own little way has changed my mindset. It has given me hope, and it made me realize that sharing was the way for me to think and feel rich.

After graduating from university, I continued my monthly commitment of sponsoring my child's education. It has been seventeen years since I first became a child sponsor, and I can truly say that I have been blessed with an amazing life. With several books under my belt, a thriving writing career, and a happy personal life, I can say that I am living the life that I have always wanted. And that is because I learned how to share my blessings to those in need.

I chose to write self-help books because I wanted to help others through my own insights, stories, and experiences. I wanted to share how it was when I was growing up, and how I was able to help myself overcome challenges and struggles. I did go through some challenges which were discouraging, but I chose to carry on. The systems that worked for me were shared in my books, and I am proud to say that I am sharing my knowledge because I want others to become more self-aware and wise. My books can provide healing and inner peace. And if I can show others that it is okay to be alone and fulfilled, then I can say that I am making a difference in this world, one book at a time.

You have the power to share what you have. You have made it this far in your life, and you have reached the end of this book. I encourage you to share what you have to those in need. Share what you have learned from this book to those who are in need of wisdom and strength. Be a friend to those who need love and care. Be a guiding light in the world that we live in. You have the power to show other people their true worth by knowing first how worthy you are of being a shining light. Share and be a blessing to others. And continue to live a life filled with happiness and strength, because you are worthy and worth it!

Thank you for reading this book, and I hope that I have helped you see how amazing you truly are.

About the Author

Samantha Gail B. Lucas

Samantha Gail B. Lucas has been blogging on her website, www.speakoutsam.com, since May 2017. She has since attended several conferences, workshops, and networking opportunities through her website. She regularly shares her favorite local finds, foodie adventures, charitable advocacies, and media partnerships. She graduated with an AB Humanities degree from the University of Asia and the Pacific. *Worthy and Worth It* is her fifteenth published book. She currently resides in Quezon City, Philippines.

www.ingramcontent.com/pod-product-compliance
Lightning Source LLC
LaVergne TN
LVHW041552070526
838199LV00046B/1929